A Greenish Man

First published 1979 by Pluto Press Limited
Unit 10 Spencer Court, 7 Chalcot Road, London NW1 8LH

Pluto Plays gratefully acknowledges financial assistance
from the Calouste Gulbenkian Foundation, Lisbon, with
the publication of this series

ISBN 0 86104 213 1

Series editor: Catherine Itzin
Cover designed by Marsha Austin
Printed in Great Britain by Latimer Trend & Company Ltd Plymouth

Snoo Wilson

A Greenish Man

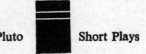

Pluto Short Plays

A NOTE ON THE AUTHOR

Snoo Wilson received the John Whiting Award for 1978 for *The Glad Hand*, his seventh full-length play (also published by Pluto Press). Others include *The Pleasure Principle* performed at the Royal Court in 1973, published by Eyre Methuen; *Pignight* and *Blowjob* published by John Calder (Publishers) Ltd; *Vampire* for Portable Theatre, *The Beast* for the Royal Shakespeare Company, *The Everest Hotel*, all of which have been published in *Plays & Players*. *Soul of the White Ant* is published by TQ Publications Ltd.

A Greenish Man

A Greenish Man is also a film for television. The central character restrains himself from action in any direction, and in the end this fragile stasis of a violent inarticulate man destroys him. The rhetoric of the characters is generally debased, although it is intended also to show their emotional lives. The play is not, however, a bullring where we watch the inarticulate being gored passively to death, it is a shifting labyrinth of overlapping concerns, public and private, in the middle of which lurks the destroying Minotaur. In the end, the central character is denuded of any possible role and so goes into oblivion in a strange state of emotional virginity.

I extended the script for the stage version printed here and was able to restore the character of Jane a little who had been elbowed to the side through successive drafts, in spite of a giant imaginative biography. The play also addresses itself to the idea of sacrifice to a political movement, in this case the IRA, in whose cause one of the villains of the piece has lost some limbs. It uses, with some joy at times, the structure of the B Movie. If I were introducing a novel, of course I should not dare point out the striking features to the onlooker. It is just that I do not want to clutter the particular performer with a set of 'ideal' stage directions as to the interpretations of good, colloquial equivocation: the text should carry the burden of ambiguity, though I am never quite sure that it does. So here, equivocally, is your man himself. Sir! Madam – *A Greenish Man*.

Snoo Wilson

A Greenish Man was first performed at the Bush Theatre on 20 November 1978. The cast was as follows:

Troy Philips	Paul Kember
George	Shay Gorman
Deirdre	Elizabeth McKelvey
O'Malley	Dudley Sutton
Young Man	James Coyle
Jane	Julia Schofield
Marwood	Richard Parmentier
Patrick	Denis Lawson

Directed by Dusty Hughes
Designed by Grant Hicks

A Greenish Man was also presented on BBC TV by BBC Birmingham as 'Play of the Week' in March 1979.

Low light on all the set.

The set is in three locations which should blur into each other. Stage right is a Victorian pub, with a bar behind which GEORGE *serves. Centre stage is a suggestion of outside wasteland – spent grass rubbed away on a dirt-packed mound, and to the left without a break begins the interior of the factory, an outstandingly shabby and dirty and broken down single storey cluttered industrial process. A pump stirs a vat intermittently.* O'MALLEY'S *office is an impressive glass-fronted door with his name on it, with advertising. Behind it is a minute space barely large enough to house a typewriter. In front, a small billiard table piled with paint cans and old sheets. A sheet of tarpaulin tacked across another entrance.*

A steam pipe hisses, then a big burst of steam.

TROY *and* GEORGE *enter,* TROY *to sit at the bar and* GEORGE *to serve, swift, businesslike. As soon as* TROY *is seated he turns to the audience, takes an empty glass in his hand. Outside, distantly, a police siren.*

Troy This lively young man is not entirely Irish. Partly only, in part of the Irish persuasion.

You see, doctor, my mother was Irish. That's what did it. And then in the hospital they said something else, they said it's the lead in your blood got me fighting. In Glasgow they did tests – on the water supply. They tore the lead piping out of the Gorbals and fed it to rats. The rats ended up fighting. But I've come for compensation. I've come for a purpose. There was a certain man put lead in my brain, not with a shooter, but just as culpable. (*To bar.*) George. Hello then George.

George Hello. What d'you want now?

Troy Pint.

GEORGE *gets it.*

D'you remember me?

George Sorry?

Troy I said, d'you remember me?

The phone rings. GEORGE *holds up his hand to* TROY. *He listens into the phone.*

George No, I'll pay for the call. Where are you? Round the corner?

Voice at the other end.

George Sainsbury's is closed on Mondays.

Voice.

George Spar. Try Spar. This is a posh do – you can't have Tesco's luncheon meat.

Voice.

George The old jew man does hands of pork, nothing else, they're too expensive. We need fifteen pound of cured ham in one piece, Deidre will tell you where to get it. She came with me last time.

Voice.

George She's *not* with you? Well where the bloody hell is she then? All right I'll find her. I'll find her. Look, I think I can hear the pips coming, I'll see you later – ta ta –

Puts the phone down.

You haven't seen a young child, about eight – ?

Troy Deidre? No.

George She's run off again.

Troy I've been damaged. Industrially damaged by O'Malleys. I had six months remedial treatment trying to get the lead out of my brain. Does O'Malley still drink here?

George He'll be in any minute.

Troy D'you remember me? Troy.

George (*pause*) Yes, I remember you, Troy. (*Shouts.*) Deidre! Deidre!

Troy Did they say why I had gone into hospital?

GEORGE *dries his hands on a tea towel and exits behind* TROY.

George (*sotto voce*) If she'd gone out with her mother like she said –

Open door. Noises of the street. TROY *hunched at bar.* DEIDRE *appears and stands on one leg looking at* TROY, *behind.*

TROY *suddenly drops his straight pint glass on the floor.*

As if the noise wakes him, he looks up with a start to see DEIDRE.

Troy D'you remember me, Deidre? I've been away in a big white hospital Bigger than the house of a millionaire.

Deidre What's that?

GEORGE *runs back in and catches* DEIDRE *by the ear and smacks her on the legs and arms. She shrieks.*

George You lying little minx. You wait till your mother comes back. Go to the bedroom! Go on!

DEIDRE *stares him out before leaving.*

Troy (*abstracted*) It wasn't because of domestic violence I went in ... It wasn't because of that, I never touched the wife. She'll tell you that herself, although with one blow I could've freed myself from her, for *life*. I'm not free. I wrote her letters but she'd moved on.

He sorts a pile of letters out on the counter. DEIDRE *exits.*

George (*looking at broken glass*) How did that happen? Was it her? (*He starts to clear it up.*) I'll get you a fresh one.
Troy It was my illness.

TROY *looking at letters,* GEORGE *clearing up.*

O'MALLEY *steals in behind the bar and takes a bottle of Guinness, and a glass.*

Sits at a table. Reaches under the table and takes the top off the bottle and pours it, all the time reading THE SUN.

Sticks a 'Sweet Afton' in his mouth, finds an empty box of matches, relaxes, reads.

He is huge, seedy, elderly, small hat, dirty suit with green paint stains all over it.

GEORGE *gets* TROY *a fresh pint.* TROY *offers to pay for it.*

George I won't hear of it.

He indicates O'MALLEY, *and gives* TROY *a box of matches.*

TROY *goes and sits down with the matches.* O'MALLEY *just sitting there with a wet cigarette in his mouth.*

GEORGE *goes back to polishing glasses.* TROY *gets out a match, lights it.*

Still nothing from O'MALLEY.

The match burns down to TROY'S *fingers. As it extinguishes,* O'MALLEY *looks up. He takes the box.*

O'Malley Thank you.
Troy I should kill you. I was a musician. Happily married man. Now, I can't play the riffs any more. Doctors, specialists, told me it was because of you.

O'MALLEY *trembling slightly as he lights his cigarette. Pause. Looks at it in his hand.*

O'Malley Pardon?
Troy Six months in hospital. I tried to do away with myself, I felt so miserable. You poisoned me.
O'Malley Excuse me?

Troy I worked over the road in your bloody paint factory.
O'Malley Yes?
Troy And I was poisoned. Lead poison. In the brain.
O'Malley I don't remember. Wait. You were the boy fell in the old paint.
Troy I could take you to court.
O'Malley Yes now, the doctors wrote to me about your condition. Not a legal matter.
Troy My memory's bad. I get blackouts. Spells of deafness then everything gets loud again. I can prove it. Here are my case notes.

O'MALLEY *takes a bundle of papers and lays them gently in the beer lying on the table.*

O'Malley Is that so?
Troy They weren't saying I was damaged to flatter me. Every word in there is fact. I know that because I nicked them. Every word is true.

O'MALLEY *glances at the papers in passing.*

There is lasting damage from titanium salts. Did you read that bit? There were titanium salts in the paint along with the lead.
O'Malley (*carefully*) In the old paint. Lead, titanium.
Troy So what are you going to do in the way of compensation?
O'Malley I don't know . . . you come rushing all over me –
Troy I think about ten thousand would settle it. Loss of memory. Premature ageing. It's all down here in black and white. You can't wriggle out of it.
O'Malley I can't give it to you. I'm bankrupt. Wreckers in the plant. It started as a small matter with the catholics asking to be paid more than the protestants because they had bigger families. A boy was killed in a brawl outside and since then I've had terrible trouble with the owd' ghost.

I've not been able to employ a soul for months. Someone gets in at night and lets the vats pour out all over the floor. I've had the police in but they can't do nothing. It's the owd' ghost. No-one won't work there, not any more. Because of the fear. Not like you. Damaged in the brain. You're not afraid.
Troy I'm afraid of nothing. I've told you what I want.
O'Malley Afraid of nothing . . . I've no money as such. I had looked forward to retiring, a little farm outside Macroom, anywhere six hundred miles away from George would 'a done.
Troy I thought George was separate from the factory.
O'Malley Does he look like me? No.

They look at GEORGE. *Hand shakes slightly.*

He's a half-brother. He was conceived the night the Inshegheela battalion of the IRA visited Macroom. I'll call him bastard to his face one day. Before this bloody shaking is the end of me. D'you think I've got that Parkinsons Disease? With your recent medical experience you . . . It goes away after a couple . . . (*Indicates beer.*) Sure, it must have been some lascivious semite seduced our dear mother, for God loves the Irish but he gave the Jews the money. (*Stands.*) Come over to the office, we'll see if we can do right by you. Are you – do you have any Irish blood in you by the way?

Troy Some, half. My mother was Irish.

O'Malley Ah, that's the way of it. If there'd been any justice the old mother would have been past it.

The YOUNG MAN *comes in. Dark dirty jacket, T shirt, intense stare at* TROY.

TROY *staring at him.*

O'MALLEY *takes* TROY *by the arm. Breaks the stare.*

See you George.

GEORGE *waves in a friendly, professional way.*

TROY *and* O'MALLEY *leave.*

The phone rings.

GEORGE *picks it up after staring at the* YOUNG MAN.

George (*to* YOUNG MAN) One moment.

The voice at the other end talks.

That's all right, sir, we didn't want any butlers. Absolutely no butlers at all. Just the cake. You have me atlas? If you can't find the Gaeltacht areas on the map, just do the whole lot green. Ulster as well. You wouldn't happen to know where I could get a leg of ham. Sainsbury's is closed on Mondays. Thank you.

YOUNG MAN *sitting at the vacated table.*

Young Man You're going to need another lookout. From where I have to be, they could get to within fifty yards and be out of sight still.

GEORGE *takes money out of the till and gives it to him.*

That's too much. Ten quid should be all right for the afternoon. Try and cut down on the overheads.

Exits. GEORGE *puts his head in his hands. Music.* DEIDRE *comes in and stands watching.*

George Pineapple juice, madam?

He pours one out for her. She drinks it slowly.

MARWOOD *and* JANE *enter,* MARWOOD *first.* GEORGE *pulls* DEIDRE *behind the bar.*

MARWOOD, *a tall lanky American,* JANE *very English, middle class, short-cropped hair. They leave cases by the table.* JANE *sits.* MARWOOD *straight to the bar.*

Marwood Two cold lagers and we need some food. Is that the extent of your sandwich selection? OK forget everything except the lagers.

GEORGE *gives them.*

D'you have the other half of this dollar bill?

George No. That's forty pence. (*To* DEIDRE.) Call me if they need anything.

Exits. DEIDRE *disappears behind bar.*

Marwood When did you separate from your husband.
Jane Six months ago. (*Pause.*) After he beat me up.
Marwood And he went into hospital afterwards rather than you?
Jane He had a choice, hospitalisation or he'd be charged with assault.
Marwood You mean he had to decide if he was mad or just bad.
Jane The booze got to his brain, too.
Marwood Booze doesn't damage your brain. Norman Mailer is one of the great American novelists and he –
Jane – is a pig.
Marwood Dylan Thomas. Drunk from the age of three. Now you're not going to tell me he didn't write great poetry with his brain.

Pause.

I'm sorry, we're arguing again. I'm sorry.
Jane I've been here before.
Marwood This is the only house still standing in the street. It's got to be here.
Jane It can't be.
Marwood I'll ask.

Turns to the bar. DEIDRE *stands on a chair and appears in view.*

She smiles.

Hi . . .

Sits again.

I don't think somehow that that's the head of the Kilburn division IRA. I can't believe it. We're in the wrong place *again.*
I can't *believe* it . . .

Picking up the bags and exiting.

Come on –

Cross fade to the factory.

O'MALLEY *taking in his property for* TROY's *benefit.*

The walls are covered with graffiti. Broken paper sacks of dye. Huge pipes running overhead and out through the doors at the back.

O'Malley He's been at it again. He sets booby traps, one week he put dog's mess in the pay packets, something worse in the tea. You can see what the problem is.

They move towards the office. Stop.

Would you like the lease as compensation? It has ten years to run, if it doesn't burn down.

Troy I want money.

O'Malley Yes, yes, absolutely correct. (*Pause.*) Did you know I've a paint here, a green paint, which you can make out of grass clippings.

TROY *smiles.*

I'd make a fortune with it myself if I was a proper practical man. D'you not want to know further about it? You could stay here and make it. All you've got to do is to get rid of the owd ghost. If you kept the name of the place, too, you'd stay lucky. What's your last name?

Troy Philips.

O'Malley Philips, that's electronics. You'd have to change your name a little if you was making paint.

Troy What to?

O'Malley O'Malley. It's a sentimental point. You see when my son was killed in the great explosion I had no-one to hand on to in the family. George is already clawing at my back for the lease . . .

Troy Isn't he an O'Malley?

O'Malley Ha! His *name's* O'Malley. If that means anything. It might have been a priest. Jesuit. At a certain age they all get so it's either Punch or Judy. I have seen in the entrance to hovels in the Wicklows, reincarnated in a three year old, the face of a familiar priest . . . It must have been a priest. Whoever it was had to have preternatural powers of inducing parturition . . . She was past it. Besides he doesn't look like anyone in the family. It *was* the priest.

Produces a big yellow envelope.

Here. The formula is all in here.

Troy (*takes it*) I know all about paint. I worked here.

O'Malley The latter day processes of paint manufacture. You have a grounding in the art. But it's nothing like that. (*Points.*) That'll be your main power source now. Sunlight. The one thing that George won't be able to take from you. Everything else, he'll try. Remember, the best paint is made under sunlight.

Troy Why don't you go and make it on a new industrial estate or something in Northampton. You'd get a bit more sunlight then.

O'Malley What, in Northampton? No. Besides, George'd think I had something worth stealing.

Troy I am right, aren't I, in thinking that this process isn't working at the moment. It's bloody useless. It's not worth a fart.

O'MALLEY goes to a smart new fridge by the office and pulls out a polythene sack full of frozen grass. He turns on some floodlights over a low tank.

O'Malley We'll have to cheat a little on this. I had expected better weather. I can scarcely make a hundred gallons a day this cursed dull summer. (*Throws the contents of the sack in.*) In goes the frozen grass. This bit is pure magic, though it's dull enough grass from Welwyn Garden City. The fibre dissolves and the chlorophyl is held in suspension till it multiplies – (*Pours from a big jug.*) This is your nutrient coming in now.

Troy What is it?

O'Malley It's an acetic acid base. You can fix nitrogen chemically but the bacteria'll do it cheaper, that's what the chlorophyl eats. Then into the next stage which is a resin stabiliser.

Here is some finished product . . .

Produces a fluorescent green shimmering spoonful from another vat.

. . . ten litres from a hundredweight of clippings.

Troy (*sceptical*) I see.

O'MALLEY tries to paint over a slogan with the green paint.

TROY looks at a paint tin label.

'O'Malley's famous stirabout paint. Only one application required.'

The office is smoking. TROY sees it first.

Troy What's that?

O'Malley (*rushing in*) Oh my god –

He beats it out in the tiny office, getting dirty in the process. He finally comes out with small cylinder on a coal shovel.

A small incendiary device. I'm surprised he doesn't drop the big one, and finish us off. Two jerrycans of petrol and a stick of dynamite. Except he'd have nowhere to live.

Troy (*about the paint*) Does this really work?

O'Malley The Irish are the most inventive race in the world, because the most abstract from the life of everyday experience. Essential for a true inventor. To be not really there when you're talking to him. Einstein, called by his teachers a lazy dog, was a mathematician who discovered an invention to do with atoms because he was not a physicist bound by conventional ideas.

Troy He wasn't Irish.

O'Malley De Valera when in prison, spent the whole of his time working out proofs of Euclidean geometry.

Smoke comes welling out of the doors at the back: the fire is out of sight.

Would you mind going this time?

TROY *nods. He runs off at the back. Burning noises and smoke increase.*

O'MALLEY *peeps round the corner.*

(*To himself.*) Jesus, that's a corker. (*Shouts.*) Are you all right, there?

The smoke increases.

Are you all right? Troy, my son, come out –

Finally TROY *emerges. His jacket off. It is in flames.* O'MALLEY *snatches it from him and stamps it out.*

Troy (*filthy, gasping*) It's no good, it's getting bigger –

O'MALLEY *snatches up a bucket and dips it into the tank of finished green paint. A thick, slimy bright green. Crackling noises increase, off.*

No.

O'MALLEY *rushes off and there is a splash off. He returns with the empty bucket. The smoke, the crackling have all ceased.*

O'Malley Thank you, sir, for what you have done. I'm sorry I waited so long, but it breaks my heart to throw the stuff away.
Troy That puts it out?
O'Malley Yes . . . well . . . liquid grass . . .

He throws the burnt jacket over his shoulder like a cloak and shrugs in a careless, magnificent way.

Fast fade.

Lights on pub side. Curtains drawn, dark, sun outside. Enter GEORGE *behind bar and* DEIDRE *in front.* DEIDRE *clutching a big china carthorse.*

George Where d'you think you're going with that, young miss? That's from the table upstairs for the supper.

Pause.

Go and put it back. I'll tell your mother.
Deidre Patrick wants it.
George Don't you start lying to me.
Deidre He does, he does. He told me to come and get it.

Enter O'MALLEY *and* TROY, *dirtier than ever.* DEIDRE *senses an advantage.*

Can I take it to him?

George (*retreating*) Who? Yes . . . all right.

DEIDRE *leaves.*

O'Malley (*sitting*) Historical truth comes from *the heart.* De Valera said
   when he wanted to know what the Irish people were thinking he only
   had to look into his own heart. (*Baring the space over his heart with
   difficulty.*) In his heart, he had a map of the passions, the persuasions, the
   oppression and chronic starvation, the neglect, the self hatred, everything that had gone before in his country. Every massacre. Every razed
   city. Nowadays it's all bureaucrats and Value Added Taxation. They
   don't believe in governments with hearts.

George Would you like to take yourself off and have a bath?

O'Malley Troy?

George Not him. You. I want a word with the sorcerer's apprentice.

O'MALLEY *stands and exits.*

GEORGE *puts a cloth over the taps.*

Troy Are you closed? I didn't know what time it was. There are two kinds of
   people. Those with watches and those without.

George Well now.

Troy What time are we living in?

George How does the old place seem to you?

Troy I mean who are we doing this for? Why are we striking all these atti-
   tudes? What time is it?

GEORGE *gives up for the moment and switches the television on.*

George D'you follow the horses?

Troy Yeah.

George I've got ten quid each way on Madam Butterfly at Redcar.

Troy There was this group of opera singers taking opera around and they
   were laughed at by the yokels, a hundred years ago, till the lead tenor
   stopped the orchestra and said to the audience, 'Gentlemen! This is
   the nineteenth century!' (*Pause.*) Gentlemen . . . this is the nineteenth
   century.

George You've been made an offer.

Switches the TV sound off.

Troy Sounds daft.

George That's what I thought when I first heard about it. Jesus, if God had
   intended the world to go that way the Garden of Eden would've been
   finished in Dulux.

Troy I wanted cash.

George A cash operation for the whole thing. Neat and tight. You could
   clean the place up and run it on proper lines.

Troy No, cash and split.

George (*canny*) You have to prove your disablement. (*Pause. Helpful.*)
   There's a certain amount of vandalism at the moment. You just need to

be firm. My brother isn't firm. In fact you've probably seen from the slogans, the damage recently appears to have put on political colours in order to disguise itself. When he asked you to take it on, were there any conditions?

Troy He wanted me to get rid of the ghost.

George Were those his very words? That's a turn up for the books. You to get rid of the ghost. What did you say?

Troy I didn't say anything.

George Well what do you think then? You've nothing to lose. Give it a whirl, try it for a month.

Troy He wants me to change my name.

George I'll let you have two fifty out of the till to get yourself cleaned up. We can't have a managing director looking like that.

Troy I don't want to change my name.

George I'll straighten out all that side of it. He's an old man, it's always been a family firm you know. It's a chance for you to make a killing in everlasting paint. For that's what it is. The more the sun shines on it, the greener it gets. It doesn't fade, and pass away. But the first part is not going to be a doddle. It'll need a hard man, with his wits about him.

Troy Is that me then?

George That's the spirit. I'm getting sick and tired of this whole business. For God knows how long, we've been looking for a new face, a new idea, a new broom to sweep out all the old rubbish, all the old prejudices, and if you can get it to work, well then, the best of luck to you, health, wealth, happiness – are you a married man? Your wife will be pleased to know. We'll firm up the deal later. This will be a rare adventure.

DEIDRE *comes in.* GEORGE *emptying till, giving* TROY *money.*

Come on, we're going shopping, madam. (*To* TROY.) Help yourself to a drink.

Holding DEIDRE *by the hand.* MARWOOD *and* JANE *come in.*

Jane (*to* MARWOOD) I won't walk any further.

George We're closed.

Jane I am going to sit here – for five minutes – in the shade. If you want to get rid of me, you're going to have to throw me out. I used to be a resident three houses down if that makes any difference.

George Five minutes.

Troy I'll lock up.

GEORGE *and* DEIDRE *exit.*

Marwood Could we have a glass of water.

TROY *turns the TV up.*

Troy Sure.

He pours them glasses of water, ice. Then he sits down to watch the TV, it's the racing.

Marwood See? We even get ice. Not very much ice, but ice.

Jane Marwood, if we're going to go to this dinner tonight assuming we can find it and it exists, we are going to have to get one or two things straightened out.

Marwood Talk.

Troy Oh my god, it's the wife.

She doesn't hear him.

Jane As far as I can see there's no point in talking to you if you're as fucking insensitive as you've been to me.

Marwood Look, if I drink a bottle of Chablis and I lie on this warm grass –

Jane A demolition site –

Marwood OK, a demolition site . . . The sun is shining. I thought we had a relationship. I'm sorry. I didn't realise you were uptight about giving head.

Jane There was a boy with binoculars – *watching*.

Marwood He wasn't a pervert.

Jane Look what is this dinner anyhow.

Marwood This guy gave me the address when I met him in the Inn on the Park. He just had my name. I dunno why.

Jane He just had your name?

Marwood Yeah, well when I was at Berkeley we used to raise a lot of bread for the Irish Republican Army. So when I got approached I naturally assumed the dinner was going to be in Ireland. I never guessed it would be here.

Jane You thought Kilburn was in Ireland?

Marwood Right.

Jane What do you know about the IRA?

Marwood They're patriots.

Jane I was engaged to someone in the IRA once. I broke it off because I couldn't face living with a killer. Which part of the IRA did you send the money to? The Officials? The Provisionals?

Marwood I dunno, we just sent it. We had an Irish bar, and we used to sell slogans you could put on your fender, or on your Honda fuel tank. Look I've got Irish blood in me, right up to here.

Jane I want to go home.

Marwood Jane. Seriously . . . I used to run a softball team in Berkeley, once a week. Not for the students but for the dropouts. No-hopers, burnt-out speed freaks, whole spectrum of street people. But every week they'd turn up on time for the game. Guys who were into total urban warfare, and guys who were just into silence. Guys who hadn't looked at a clock for years. All I'm saying is that if we wait here, we'll make our connection, because the dedicated player always comes.

Jane I didn't know you were into social work.

Marwood I wasn't born a tax lawyer, you know.

JANE *laughs abruptly.*

Jane You managed to drop in to society again.

TROY *sits up.*

Just a minute . . . Troy! What are you doing here?

Troy (*pause*) I'm waiting for the baseball to begin.

Jane Have you been listening?

Troy No, just got one of my spells of deafness. (*To* MARWOOD.) Nice to see you're getting to know all the aspects of the wife.

Marwood Were you two together.

Jane Yes, but he had a court order to stop molesting me. It's because you're sick. Fortunately, when he fell in the paint we had some kind of excuse for a dignified separation.

Troy It's all right, I'm better now, I've been treated by the National Health. It's a great system, mate, it's like sex for women. They may not like it at first, but once they start, they can't leave off.

Jane He was too sick for direct personal relationships.

Troy Right, you don't get those in hospitals. I married Jane because she was arty – her mother runs a gallery.

Jane He was marrying the middle class.

Troy We moved here because Jane thought it was a real working-class area. She was right. They bulldozed it.

Jane Troy says that I was brought up on all those stories about virile sons of toil and I was marrying the working class.

Marwood Look, the class system in this country is a closed book to me. I think you're both crazy.

Jane No.

Troy No. Look, it's all right, I'm gentle as a lamb. I had my illness recognised, as an industrial illness. And in addition to monetary compensation I've been given the key to a brand new ecological way of paint manufacture . . .

He hasn't got his jacket on. The hand goes to the jacket pocket.

I've left it over the road. So people won't ever have to be damaged again . . . we'll all be rich – see? O'Malley gave it to me. It's . . .

Jane What is it?

Troy It's a secret process for making cheap green paint. Out of grass.

Marwood Green paint . . . maybe we have come to the right place after all.

Troy It's in my jacket. Don't go –

Exits.

JANE *makes a deliberate and obvious advance to* MARWOOD. *He hands her off.* JANE *teasing him.*

Marwood I love you too – but . . . isn't he coming back?
Jane Come on. Don't be afraid.
Marwood Honey he's going to walk right in on us – –
Jane I'll make it quick –

MARWOOD *sits watching the horse racing.* JANE *obscured by a table digging in his flies.*

MARWOOD *stands.*

Marwood You do want him to find us. I'm not going to play that game.
Jane Fine.

MARWOOD *doing up his flies.*

The YOUNG MAN *comes in.*

Marwood You were in the street above us, weren't you. Would you satisfy our curiosity? We were just wondering if you were a pervert.

The YOUNG MAN *frisks them, for weapons, against the bar. The* YOUNG MAN *empties the suitcases on the ground. Out fall evening dress, expensive talcum and shaving gear for* MARWOOD, *nighties with frills for* JANE.

He goes through the cases, slowly.

You are a pervert.
Young Man Just looking.
Marwood What for?
Young Man Shorts.
Marwood There you are.
Young Man Guns, to you.
Marwood You just stop people in the street and search them?
Young Man Round here I do. You wouldn't thank me now, would you if one of the other guests brought a bomb.
Marwood You're to do with the dinner?
Young Man You're a bit early, for dinner.
Marwood Yes I . . .
Jane Thought we were going to Dublin till he looked at the address.

YOUNG MAN *jamming the clothes back into the cases.*

Would you mind folding them *properly*?
Young Man (*stands up*) Yes well . . . I never got in the way of all that. I only had one lot of clothes, and I slept in them, when I was a kid. Why don't you go for a walk for a couple of hours and come back here.
Marwood Just a minute. Check. Do you have the other half of . . . (*Produces it.*) . . . this dollar bill?

YOUNG MAN *looks at it closely. Lights fading fast.*

Young Man No.

The factory.

O'MALLEY *slumped on the 'bed' sweating. Panting.*

TROY *entering.*

O'Malley Troy, my son. Jesus, it's a hot day. Hot as a bitches arse. Fancy a bit of firewatching?

Troy I've come for my jacket.

TROY *looking in his jacket for the plans.*

O'Malley I thought you were getting a new one.

Troy Where are the papers?

O'Malley What papers? What is yous talking around?

Troy Oh, sod it. (*Turns to go.*)

O'Malley Wait! (*Jumps up.*) Did you not take money from George?

Troy Yes.

O'Malley Well how much did you sell my processing secret for that you should be pretending it's gone?

Troy I didn't.

O'Malley Look I'm not daft in the head like you. I am afraid of some things.

Troy He gave me compensation, that's all.

O'Malley It is no business of his. That old woman, with his fine silk shirts on his back, and his wife laden with suffering oysters, and his trips abroad ... (*Pause.*) I gave you the one gift of my life which made it worthwhile, I gave it to you as my *son*. Because I don't have one. I don't have a son. Just the owd, ghost.

Troy (*exiting, sarcastic*) Maybe the ghost took the papers.

Pause.

O'Malley Of course ...

Troy Yes ...

O'Malley Well now. That's the way of it. He'd be jealous. He'd love to start a scrap between the two of us. *That's* it ... How the hell do we get it back off him?

A polite cough, behind. TROY *turns, through a tarpaulin flap, a hideous wizened figure on a trolley, legless, the face covered in scars. A punting-pole in its hands, relaxed. Alert eyes. The whole streaked and daubed with green.*

Patrick Race you for it.

O'Malley (*resigned*) Here he is. The servant and instigator of strife himself. Patrick, this is Troy.

Patrick Here. Catch.

Throws TROY *a china horse.* TROY *catches it and holds it.*

PATRICK *holds out his hand for the horse.*

TROY *puzzled gives it back.*

See that, father? His reflexes look all right to me. Still, these spongers off the welfare state will go to any lengths to prove –

O'Malley Did you take the papers from his jacket?

Patrick It's my invention. Has he been posing as the chemical genius? The green paint is just a sideshow. I make explosives. Did you know you can make explosives out of almost anything? Flour? Butter? We found from experiment, it's best to give the troops the inedible ones. And since the English tightened up on quarries I even do a neat little detonator. My signature tune. No bigger than that. (*Finger and thumb.*)

O'Malley Watch what you're saying.

Patrick He's one of us, isn't he?

Troy My . . . mother was Irish. (*Glazed.*)

Patrick No, but are you of our persuasion.

Troy (*pause*) Yes.

Patrick Would you go and help George with the supper, father. I want to talk to this boy alone.

O'MALLEY *leaves, humiliated.*

Married?

Troy A long time ago.

Patrick I was adored once, too. Before my accident. But it concentrated the mind wonderfully. I'm writing about the old country. There's no such thing I found as a short history of Ireland, so I'm writing a long one. The rest of the time I invent, and make bombs.

Troy What kind of bombs?

Patrick (*patient*) Explosive bombs. Ones that go '*bang*' under British soldiers. (*Pause. Firm.*) I need the place to myself. George makes enough money to support father. I'd *hate* to move.

Troy George and your father are not politically active then?

PATRICK *shakes head.*

Patrick George doesn't really worry his head about the world beyond the end of the street, and daddy's dying. It could take him twenty years, if he took cortisone, but either way it's very counter revolutionary. (*Pause.*) So. You've got brain damage . . .

Troy (*dully*) And a frustrated desire to be a musician. But, somehow . . . (*Pause.*)

Patrick Poor co-ordination? Spasms of uncontrollable rage?

Troy Yes.

Patrick Sentimental, but beats the wife. (*To the air.*) *Quoi de neuf?*

Troy Why do they talk about you as the ghost?

Patrick When I was blown up – hoist with my own petard as a matter of fact – I was listed as dead. The ultimate alibi – they thought I'd vapourised. So I'm the ghost. All that stands between you and your rightful inheritance. You see, father feels his end. He's getting soft. He wants, I'm convinced of this, to make his peace with a non-existent god. It's absurd. And he actually feels responsible for you.

Troy Well . . . isn't he?

Patrick D'you deserve something which you haven't worked for?

Troy I bloody worked.

Patrick Only a fool would have worked here. No safety guards. Poison everywhere. I thought I was making it clear I was closing the place down for good. But because I haven't any *balls* any more, O'Malley wants to renegotiate his contract with his maker by turning one of these pathetic *proles* into his bleeding son. A brain damaged one at that. An *idiot*.

Troy No mate, look, it's not that bad – just you watch it or no matter how crippled you are . . . I used to be a musician. OK?

Patrick It doesn't matter what you used to be.

Troy OK, and we all finish up with the worms too, doctors . . . doctors told me, the human brain is like the human heart, it has great capacity for repairing damage, but I never heard of anybody growing a spare set of legs.

Patrick Not a limb fall to the ground in the struggle we all love without purging the mind, strengthening the will to continue.

Troy Oh yeah?

Patrick The will is most important. As my friend Dodgson the mathematician put it, 'Will you won't you will you won't you won't you join the dance.' Because you'll be working for me. D'you want to work for me? Or them?

Troy I'll have to think about it.

Cross fade to the pub downstairs. O'MALLEY *and* GEORGE.

O'Malley You have a cheek telling me to get rid of my own son!

George What were you asking this new boy to do then? Play him at hop-scotch?

O'Malley I left it deliberately vague.

George Is he political?

O'Malley He's a lost soul. He'll come with us.

George Has he met Patrick?

O'Malley Oh, yes, oh, he'll deal with Patrick, easy.

George How?

O'Malley The boy told me himself. He has no imagination he's afraid of nothing.

George Good.

O'Malley But suppose he gets rid of Patrick and is even worse? At least Patrick only comes out at night.

George If you thought that, why did you tell him to change his name to O'Malley?

O'Malley I don't like it, keeping Patrick under lock and key like a criminal.

But you have to. Five years ago it was different, but now, if people found out what he was doing, they'd kick his brains out in the street!

George The dinners are popular.

O'Malley They make you a great deal of money.

George There's a bloody great risk involved. I have scores of lookouts posted round here for days. It cost me a thousand to set the whole thing up. As for Patrick's idea of flying in Provies to talk to the punters, it's absurd. The chances are that no one but the Special Branch will turn up and we'll be caught and bloody martyred for the price of a plate of ham –

O'Malley You're safe for this time.

George How do you know? You don't even know how to tie your bleeding shoelaces –

O'Malley The boys have closed down Dublin Airport. Your special guests have decided not to come.

George And I sent them the first-class air fares! (*Incensed.*) The bloody ungrateful bastards. Still, it makes it a bit easier to deal with Patrick, with them out the way. (*Pause.*) D'you not want to go through with it?

O'Malley I can't be a party to killing my own son.

George Cheer up, he's dead already.

O'Malley Worse, he's pinched the plans back . . .

TROY *suddenly lounging in the doorway, flashy suit, kipper tie, stepped shoes, chunky electronic watch, rings on his fingers, the very image of a would be record executive who has eschewed denim.*

George Are you coming to dinner here tonight?

Troy What kind of dinner?

George A Republican dinner.

Troy You going to blow up the houses of parliament afterwards?

George No, we're going to go home.

Troy Sounds all right.

O'Malley (*out of his depth*) Nice . . . watch you're wearing Troy.

Troy Yes, it is nice, isn't it? No tick . . . even . . . spent all the money . . . Patrick's a cold bastard. Isn't he? Good ideas though.

George You think you could make the paint thing work?

Troy No problem. (*Sniffs himself.*) Nice. What was it called? Arabis? My psychotherapist said to me, if I could become not dependent on institutions to give me an identity, it would be a significant step on the road to recovery.

George (*pause*) We were wondering if we could trust you.

Troy See for yourself.

George What d'you know about Patrick?

O'Malley He won't give up the paint formula.

Troy Yes, well then . . . It's his idea.

George You admire him?

Troy Yes. He doesn't make a whole lot of sense, but then who does?

George Plainly. If you decide to stay, he'll try to get rid of you. Unless you can defend yourself against him, in advance.

Troy Well, I always fancied myself as a bit of an ecologist. If you want me to stay, I won't take any nonsense from him. Any trouble and – boum – (*Waves his fist.*) Collapse of legless party.

George You may have to use more than a fist.

Troy I've done more than that in my time.

Change lights to red.

The O'MALLEY BROTHERS *change the set and bring on the table.*

TROY *at the back leaning on the bar. He puts on dark glasses.*

The O'MALLEY BROTHERS *bring on a long white clothed table and lay a cake and places on it.*

Music. The Dubliners 'The Black Velvet Band'.

The layout is finished, music fades.

George (*to* TROY) We think he carries a gun, but he takes some time to see things on his right side. The shovel will be behind the door of the men's. When you leave, say you have to visit the toilet.

The shovel by the toilet is illuminated in a shaft of light.

High piping noise.
The light starts to fade.

Troy (*at large*) With these men, I am united in blood, and once I have ratified that bond, I shall become fixed in their affections as a son.

Blackout.

The doors behind lit. We hear pub noises 'downstairs' as the pub becomes the upstairs dining-room.

TROY *comes forward into the action.*

O'MALLEY *and* GEORGE, *mostly the latter, assembling the table, the chairs, the cutlery.*

Troy Doesn't your wife give you a hand?

GEORGE *just looks at him.*

Deidre (*with box of cutlery*) Daddy . . . how many places?
George (*flustered*) Put them all out.

DEIDRE *laying the table.*

Deidre Knife-right. Knife-right. Knife-right. Knife-right.

The big cake with the map of Ireland on it is brought in. Candles, flowers in cupid covered vases, napkins. A big candelabra in the middle of the table.

GEORGE *turns out the lights.*

JANE *and* MARWOOD *arrive up the stairs in their full evening gear.*

O'Malley Shall I get Patrick?

George (*nods*) If he's ready.

O'Malley (*to* MARWOOD *and* JANE) Sure, isn't he always ready. (*Sits again.*) Good evening, sir, madam, could I take your coats? Would you like a drink?

Marwood White wine if it's cold. Do you have any cigars?

George Downstairs in the main bar.

MARWOOD *exits.*

Jane That's your daughter, isn't it?

George That's right.

Jane We . . . (*Indicating her and* TROY.) . . . used to live up the road. One night we were in here and she hid in the dumb waiter.

George She's always going off. She's a bad girl. Aren't you, Deidre?

Deidre Yes and I remember you, you had bruises all over your face.

Jane I . . . did. Yes. And my arms.

Deidre What happened?

Jane I fell down.

George Come on, Deidre.

GEORGE *and* DEIDRE *exit.*

Jane You didn't pay to come here did you?

Troy No . . . I'm working here now.

Jane Oh I see. That's good of them.

Troy Thanks.

Jane What are you going to do?

Troy I'm going to set up the paint factory again.

Jane But . . . isn't it just a cover for something else, that factory?

Troy There's a new process. How's your mother?

Jane Still stuck in the sixties. She's working on a fountain. She's done a maquette of me sitting in the bath, no clothes on, of course, in the act of opening a can of Coca-Cola. The water sprays out of the can and I've got this silly orgasmic expression on my face.

DEIDRE *re-enters and stands watching at the door.*

Troy (*sober*) Be nice to leave a brass copy of your body, somewhere, in a garden, in Italy.

Jane Yeah. I'm glad you're better.

Troy I'm . . . going to . . . they've asked me to get rid of a troublemaker. I'm a troubleshooter.

Jane Who?

Troy In order to claim the full compensation . . . I believe you know him.

Jane Patrick? I didn't know he was still around. Makes no odds to me. That was all a long time ago. I've moved to the right since then.

Troy It's my big break. I deserve it. But I can't do it if you're there.

Jane Do what?

Troy Get rid of him. (*Makes throat cutting gesture.*) At the dinner . . . you see they figured no-one would talk, to the police I mean, no-one would risk telling the police that they were at a fundraising dinner for the IRA . . .

Jane Don't do it.

Troy I'm too far in to quit now. You've never understood . . . I'm a Taurus, you see, I need to belong to something.

Jane I'll shop you.

Troy No.

Jane Try me.

Troy All right, I will.

> PATRICK *enters. He is walking with two sticks. Smartly dressed. Followed by Young Man.*

Patrick Hello Jane. What a surprise.

Jane Patrick? I'm sorry, I didn't recog – You look different.

Patrick I'm still me. (*Pause.*) For what it's worth. (*Sits with difficulty.*) Two things. (*To* YOUNG MAN.) Find out about the car blocking the road and I've changed my mind about Troy.

> YOUNG MAN *leaves.*

> DEIDRE *exits.*

> GEORGE, O'MALLEY, JANE *and* MARWOOD *sit at the long table.* PATRICK *has a pile of perfectly wrapped and decorated presents by his side.* TROY *turns and runs through the doors. He rushes to the illuminated lavatory. The rest of the cast freeze, their glasses in mid-air. Many empty places.*

> TROY *vomits into the lavatory. He stands up and leaves.*

> *The guests gradually unfreeze.*

Patrick Troy is going to be supervising the development of a number of projects.

> TROY *enters the room. Cannot sit down.*

> . . . Developing further some of the new paint technology.

> *Grasps* TROY *by the arm and draws him to him.*

> D'you know what I think we ought to do? I think we ought to specialise in sentimental, romantic kitsch. Horsebrasses. Garden gnomes.

> TROY *sits.*

We could be tooled up for when plaster ducks make a comeback. You and I.

TROY *stands.*

Troy Excuse me . . . I don't feel well. (*Emphasis.*) I have to visit the toilet. (*Exits.*)

Patrick We don't need to wait.

They start to eat.

Marwood Where are the hotshots?

Patrick We've just received a message saying they've been delayed. You can address any questions you like to me.

Marwood The IRA is losing its base, isn't it?

Patrick It hasn't all been plain sailing.

Marwood Why d'you do it? Kill people?

Patrick I never admired the man, but Marx was fond of quoting Hegel. 'The owl of Minerva take its flight in the evening.' Wisdom comes as night falls. We sometimes find we have to bring on the night.

TROY *re-enters and sits at a different place.*

The lights change. Music comes swelling up – 'The Black Velvet Band'. The lights go up to normal. The table is full of dirty dishes.

Patrick This phase of the struggle is now in its tenth year, and it has become more and more difficult to recruit sympathisers, particularly in this country, of sufficient political calibre. In Eire, we can rely on young men before they are married, finding the patriot cause more attractive than the dole queue. But we can't offer wages on a par with the SAS and the young men and women often drift away. It has the advantage of keeping the movement young. Your companion was a great sympathiser in the days when the civil rights movement was riding on the back of our army. Since then for her, we've rather gone out of fashion. The money that used to come from the American campuses is drying up for the same reason. Money is more important than sympathy. We've been unpopular before now. But we still get our English recruits, don't we Troy? Men who aren't afraid to put their hand in the fire. Men whose anger, whose pride cuts like a thermal lance through the pride, the hypocrisy of the British State.

Marwood So I guess you're finding it difficult.

TROY *rushes out again.*

Goes to lavatory. Seizes the shovel. A long-handled Irish one. Covered in dust and cobwebs.

DEIDRE *is brought in. She has traditional Irish dancing dress and pumps on.*

She mounts the table to dance in the middle of it, to recorded fiddle music. Everybody gradually starts to clap.

TROY *re-enters with the shovel, and is about to brain* PATRICK *when* DEIDRE *sees him. She stops dancing, and people stop clapping.* TROY *rushes out of the room again before they can turn round.*

DEIDRE *resumes the dance.*

She finishes. Applause.

Patrick Please . . . Open your *gifts.*

Everyone opens the green tissue wrapped package in front of them. Inside each of them is an identical china carthorse.

(*To* DEIDRE.) You'll get yours later. (*She doesn't go.*) Run along . . .

Pause.

DEIDRE *runs off suddenly, upset.*

PATRICK *stands with difficulty, puts his lecture notes in front of him.*

The patriotic war in Ulster is a war of roots. Four hundred years ago our fathers were starved or scattered so that English landlords could be planted in Irish soil. In the last fifty years great steps have been made toward ridding our soil of the oppressor. The car bomb. The incendiary device. The marksman with the Armalite rifle, are the dictators of the tenor of life in Belfast today. And wherever we are beaten back, our defences cruelly cut down, our captured army living naked in its own excrement, new troops arise, dedicated to giving their life for the cause.

Looks at notes.

And still the English ask, 'When will there be peace?' They ask for peace with their mouths, while their hands are writing death warrants for the flower of a people who will not accept under any terms their tyrannical governance. England's morality in this matter is totally bankrupt. There is world wide condemnation of the terrorism and torture which goes on in her political prisons under the name of law and order. The English believe that the Irish cause can, by suppression be rendered impotent. That they can prevent the conception of fresh troubles by making illegal the coupling of Ireland with her own beloved past. In Ireland, history is alive and she can bear fruit. In England, history is dead and the men who lie with her inseminate a corpse. Her children walk our streets in blackface, gun in hand, boot in the door, with glazed expression and dead eyes. Their politicians plough the same liberal furrow in blinkers in the apathetic English fog, resigned to the loss of all but this last piece of English Empire. The tide turned a long time ago. Before the last British soldier left American soil in 1776, most if not all of our recent troubles had been already sown. So, in history, there is truth, and there is fiction. The fiction in Ireland is rule of the oppressor. Where is truth? The truth is the dialectic process, which never stops. It simply goes underground. There is always an issue from the affairs of the day, however fruitlessly the blood of martyrs seems to be shed. In history, between thesis and antithesis, there may be delay, but there is always issue.

Music starts, distant, heroic, swelling as the YOUNG MAN *brings on the covered cage.*

There is never, finally, *impotence.*

YOUNG MAN *draws cover off cage to reveal bright green doves.* PATRICK *takes them out and passes them round to the astonished guests.* PATRICK *takes one and places it on his shoulder.*

TROY *enters and is again about to strike* PATRICK *from behind when he sees the green dove sitting on* PATRICK'*s shoulder.*

The rest of the guests don't notice.

A frenzy of indecision.

Troy Shit. Shit . . .

TROY *exits having failed. Throws the shovel down noisily outside. Pause.* JANE *gets up.*

Jane I've got to speak. To avoid something dreadful happening. I don't like you Patrick, I'm afraid of you, I despise what you stand for . . . but you ought to know. Troy's going to come back into this room and kill you. None of us are supposed to say anything because of why we're here. He's got to be stopped. (*Sits down.*) Marwood will you stop him.

Marwood Of course. (*Exits.*)

Patrick Who . . . suggested this to him?

Jane I . . . don't know. He just told me he had to do it.

O'Malley Dear god and this a man you were going to take under your wing too, Patrick.

George It was an actual threat of violence?

Jane Yes. In fact he said you two . . . (O'MALLEY *and* GEORGE) . . . set him up to it.

George What? In my own house?

O'Malley (*pious*) It's like a *nightmare.*

Patrick He seemed . . . ill. Nothing else.

MARWOOD *re-enters.*

Marwood I can't find him. Look, these big shots aren't coming, are they?

Pause.

George Well . . . no.

Marwood Four hundred bucks for this? And the food was for shit. I've been burned. Jane are you coming?

Pause.

I'm never going to give another cent to you guys. You are through and through phonies. In fact, I think I could probably sue you.

Exits.

Patrick Well, I thought it was just getting interesting.

TROY *enters.*

Troy George. Message for you. From your wife. Deidre's missing.
George Since when?
Troy Since it was dark.
George That woman . . .

GEORGE *exits. Pause.*

O'MALLEY *putting dove back in the cage.*

O'Malley D'you feel like an early night Patrick?
Patrick I hope she's alright. I got her a present.

Brings up a cage full of green doves and takes one out, from the dumb waiter.

She told me you couldn't get green doves. But you can.

O'MALLEY *pushes him past* TROY. PATRICK *stops by him.*

Here.

Gives him the yellow envelope. And a wrapped carthorse. TROY *unwraps it.*

Troy What's with the horses?
Patrick They're hollow. We're going to start making them, you and I. And shipping them to the old country. Any objections? 'He who is not with me is against me.'

Shouts of 'DEIDRE' *distantly outside.*

O'MALLEY *and* PATRICK *exeunt.*

Jane So what are you going to do?
Troy I don't know.
Jane Here's my telephone number.

She stuffs a piece of paper in his pocket.

Troy That was a brave thing to do.
Jane I'm going to look for the little girl.

Exits. Lights going fast.

TROY *looking at* PATRICK's *speech notes.*

Troy The owl of . . . Minerva . . .

Blackout. Exterior night sounds. Buses, cars, footsteps. Shouts of 'DEIDRE' *from all and sundry. But desultory.*

A slash of sodium light diagonally across the stage from above.

TROY *and* DEIDRE *advance and meet under the lamplight.*

TROY *still clutching the horse.* DEIDRE *heavily and badly lipsticked.*

Troy Hey! What have you been doing? They're all looking for you. You won't half catch it when you go home. Your uncle's got some green doves for you.

Deidre I'm not going home. I don't like it. I've met a man and he's going to take me away, because Mummy and Daddy beat me and are cruel.

Troy I think they'd miss you.

Deidre He's very tall and polite. He's my friend. Can I hold the horse?

She takes it.

Troy What man? Did he give you the lipstick?

Pause.

The horse starts to tick.

GEORGE *suddenly at a distance.*

George Deidre! Come here at once!

DEIDRE *alarmed.*

You there! Leave her alone! I'll call the police. Deidre!

DEIDRE *holding the horse out to* TROY *in despair.* TROY *not moving to take it.*

Blackout.

Explosion.

Shouts of 'DEIDRE'.

END OF PLAY